NATURE in Art

Words that appear in **bold** type are defined in the glossary on pages 28 and 29.

Please visit our web site at: **www.garethstevens.com**
For a free color catalog describing Gareth Stevens Publishing's
list of high-quality books and multimedia programs, call
1-800-542-2595 (USA) or 1-800-387-3178 (Canada).
Gareth Stevens Publishing's fax: (414) 332-3567.

Library of Congress Cataloging-in-Publication Data

Baumbusch, Brigitte.
     Nature in art / by Brigitte Baumbusch.
          p. cm. — (What makes a masterpiece?)
     Includes index.
     ISBN 0-8368-4448-3 (lib. bdg.)
     1. Nature in art—Juvenile literature.   I. Title.
N7650.B38   2005
     704.9'43—dc22   2004056565

This edition first published in 2005 by
Gareth Stevens Publishing
A WRC Media Company
330 West Olive Street, Suite 100
Milwaukee, Wisconsin 53212 USA

Copyright © Andrea Dué s.r.l. 1999

This U.S. edition copyright © 2005 by Gareth Stevens, Inc.
Additional end matter copyright © 2005 by Gareth Stevens, Inc.

Translator: Erika Pauli

Gareth Stevens series editor: Dorothy L. Gibbs
Gareth Stevens art direction: Tammy West

Printed in the United States of America

1 2 3 4 5 6 7 8 9 09 08 07 06 05

What Makes a ? Masterpiece?

NATURE in Art

by Brigitte Baumbusch

GARETH STEVENS
GS
PUBLISHING
A WRC Media Company

What makes nature ...

The designs on the body of this blue hippopotamus show the plants and birds that can be found in its **habitat**. The little **figurine** was made in Egypt more than 3,500 years ago.

a masterpiece?

The nightingale in this first-century Roman **fresco** is a **modest** little creature, but no other bird can **rival** its song.

This thirteenth-century Chinese painting on a paper **scroll** (below) **depicts** a pond and the plants and animals that live there.

Nature is vast blue oceans . . .

A boundless ocean, calm and **transparent** (left), was painted by French artist Henri-Edmond Cross at the end of the nineteenth century.

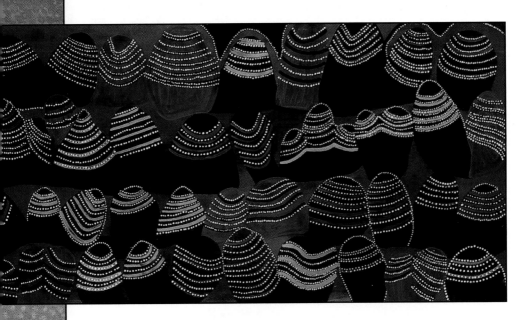

and picturesque mountains.

In contrast, vibrant colors swirl across these mountains (above), which were painted by a **contemporary Aborigine** artist from Australia. The Aborigine people are very artistic and still paint the way their **ancestors** did long ago.

Nature has many shapes...

The animals in these two simple pictures are represented in very interesting shapes.

The bird with its feathers surrounding it (right) is a Japanese ornament from the seventeenth century.

The swimming fish (below) were drawn by Swiss artist Paul Klee in the 1920s.

Gustav Klimt was an artist who lived in Vienna, Austria.
In 1907, he painted this brilliant field of **poppies** that
looks almost like a carpet.

and colors . . .

and it sparkles with light.

In the late 1800s, many French artists began working outdoors in the open air. They wanted to paint nature in a way that showed the effects of natural light. These artists were known as "Impressionists."

This picture of a pond in the woods was painted by Claude Monet, who was one of the most famous Impressionists.

Nature is both great...

High atop a mountain, the man in this picture sees a vast and majestic **landscape**. The picture was painted in the early 1800s by German artist Caspar David Friedrich.

Five hundred years ago, another German artist, Albrecht Dürer, painted a small world of grasses, in fine detail.

A grasshopper is one of nature's small details. The grasshopper to the right is a mechanical toy made in the 1920s.

and small . . .

and as full of wonder . . .

These pages contain two pictures of imaginary forests that are full of animals.

"Landscape with Yellow Birds" (below) was painted by Paul Klee in 1923.

"The Beautiful Forest" (left) is a **miniature** from a **medieval** book.

This golden **stag** (right) was made by the Scythians, an **ancient** people who lived around the Black Sea, in Russia.

as a fairy tale.

Nature can be calm . . .

A leaf-shaped dish made of **tortoiseshell** has been carved to show a pair of birds in a peaceful landscape. The carving was done in Japan in the nineteenth century.

The jungle, with its huge plants and wild animals, is a beautiful, exciting place, but it is also frightening and dangerous. **Naive artist** Henri Rousseau painted this picture of the jungle in 1910. Rousseau had never been in a jungle, but he had seen photographs.

or wild.

Sometimes, nature is terrifying!

In this Japanese **print** by Katsushika Hokusai, a storm-tossed sea threatens the lives of the fishermen huddled in their boats. A high wave towers over the boats like an open mouth, ready to swallow them up.

People observe nature . . .

This meadow full of flowers is part of a larger painting by Sandro Botticelli, who lived in Florence, Italy, about five hundred years ago.

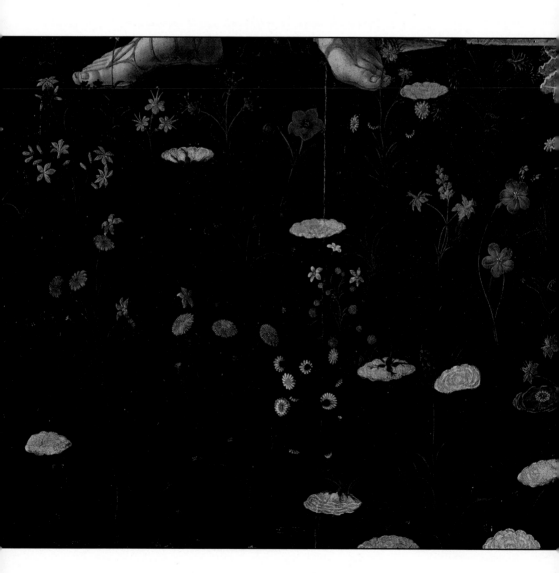

A **botanical** drawing (above) from the seventeenth century helped scientifically identify and **classify** plants and animals. The red fish beneath the drawing is a prehistoric painting from Australia. When Australian Aborigines drew animals, they often showed what the insides of the animals looked like.

study it . . .

arrange it . . .

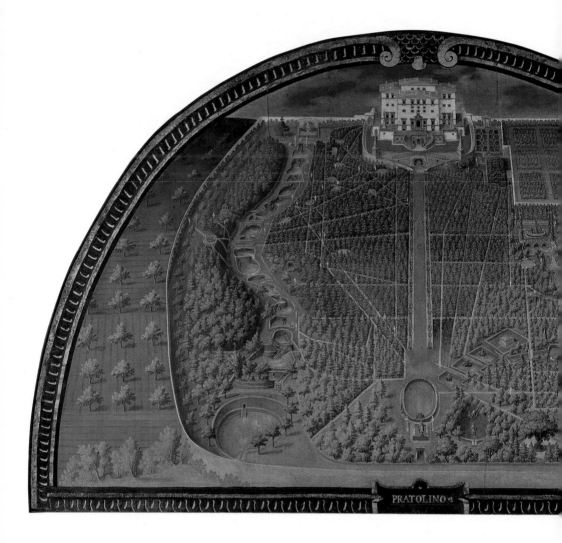

In the large garden of an Italian **Renaissance villa**, nature itself has created a work of art. Trees and other plantings combine with fountains and pools to form an **idyllic** place for leisure and relaxation.

This magnificent golden rose was ordered by a rich **lord** in the **Middle Ages** as a gift for a friend.

and imitate it.

Nature is life . . .

In this nineteenth-century painting, French artist Jean-Baptiste-Camille Corot expresses the joy in being surrounded by nature.

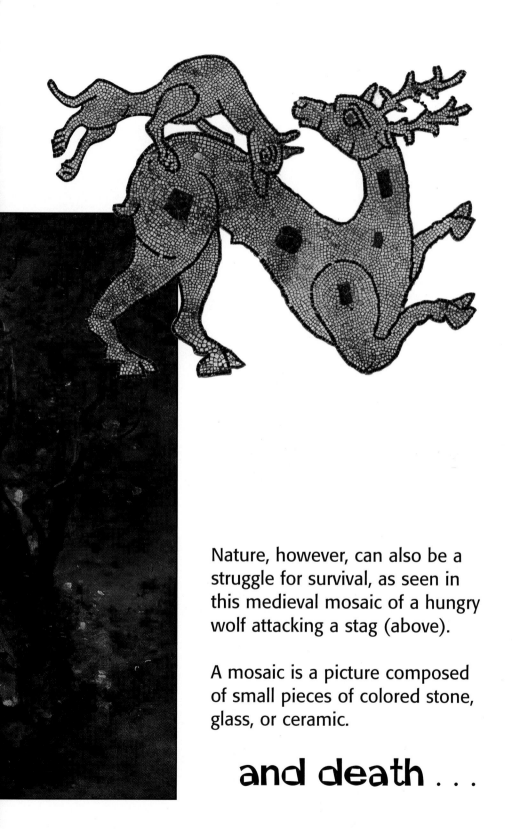

Nature, however, can also be a struggle for survival, as seen in this medieval mosaic of a hungry wolf attacking a stag (above).

A mosaic is a picture composed of small pieces of colored stone, glass, or ceramic.

and death . . .

and imagination!

In this picture from the 1960s, naive artist Ivan Rabuzin, from Croatia, created a topsy-turvy world. A tiny village is **nestled** in a flower pot with enormous flowers looking on.

GLOSSARY

Aborigine
belonging to a culture of people whose ancestors were Australia's first inhabitants

ancestors
the members of a family who lived in earlier times; past generations

ancient
relating to a period in history from the earliest civilizations until about the time of the Roman Empire

botanical
relating to botany, which is the study, or science, of plants

classify
to arrange in groups, or classes, that are based on specific characteristics

contemporary
relating to a person or an event living or happening in current or modern times

depicts
shows or describes by means of a picture

figurine
a small, decorative, statuelike figure, usually made of china, pottery, wood, or metal

fresco
a painting on a wall, specifically, a type of painting done on fresh, damp plaster, using water-based pigments (colorings) or paints

habitat
the place in nature where a particular animal or plant is commonly found

idyllic
picturesque and peaceful, having a natural or pastoral (countryside) simplicity

landscape
a wide view of the natural scenery or land forms of a particular area, which can be seen all at the same time from one place

lord
a nobleman, or man of high rank and position, in medieval times, usually one who owned large amounts of land and had power and control over everyone who lived or worked on the land

medieval
belonging to the Middle Ages

Middle Ages
a period of history in Europe from the end of the Roman Empire to the 1500s

miniature
a very small painting or a painting in an illuminated (ornately decorated with artistic lettering as well as pictures and designs in gold, silver, and bright colors) book or manuscript

modest
not bold or showy; humble, or placing only moderate value on personal attributes, abilities, and achievements

naive artist
a person with a natural ability for drawing, painting, or any other art form and who is self-taught rather than formally schooled in the rules and technical aspects of art

nestled
settled in snugly, as if in a nest

poppies
ornamental plants, some varieties of which have herbal or medicinal value. One of the best known varieties has large reddish orange flowers that produce the tiny black poppy seeds used in cooking and baking.

print
(n) a copy of an original work of art that has been reproduced through some type of printing or photographic process

Renaissance
a period of European history, between the Middle Ages (14th century) and modern times (17th century), during which learning flourished and interest in classical (relating to ancient Greek and Roman civilizations) art and literature was renewed, or "reborn"

rival
(v) to compete with or claim to equal the abilities or qualities of another

scroll
a long piece of rolled paper or paperlike material on which messages or documents were commonly written before printing and bookbinding were invented

stag
a male deer

tortoiseshell
the bony, marble-patterned substance of which some kinds of turtles' shells are made

transparent
clear enough to see through

villa
the countryside estate of a wealthy person, usually including a large house and a lot of yard and garden space

PICTURE LIST

page 4 – Faience (glazed clay) figurine of a hippopotamus. Egyptian art of the Second Intermediate Period, 18th to 17th centuries B.C. Cairo, Egyptian Museum. Drawing Studio Stalio / Andrea Morandi.

pages 4-5 – Qian Xuan (13th century): Early Autumn. Detroit, The Detroit Institute of Art. Museum photo.

page 5 – Frescoed wall with a garden scene, detail. Roman art, 1st century A.D. Pompeii, House of the Golden Bracelet. Photo Scala Archives.

pages 6-7 – Henri-Edmond Cross (1856-1910): The Golden Isles. Paris, Musée d'Orsay. Photo Giraudon / Alinari.

Jack Britten Joolama (b. 1925): Purnululu, 1983. Private property. Reproduced by courtesy of the Ebes Collection.

page 8 – Matashichi Hayashi (17th century): Sword guard, in iron, depicting a bird. Tokyo, Eisei Bunko Library. Drawing by Lorenzo Cecchi.

Paul Klee (1879-1940): Migrating Fish, 1926, pen and pencil drawing. Private property. Photo Kunstmuseum, Bern, Paul-Klee-Stiftung. © Paul Klee by SIAE, 1999.

page 9 – Gustav Klimt (1862-1918): Field of Poppies, 1907. Vienna, Österreichische Galerie Belvedere. Museum photo.

pages 10-11 – Claude Monet (1840-1926): Pond at Montgeron. St. Petersburg, The Hermitage. Photo Scala Archives.

page 12 – Caspar David Friedrich (1774-1840): Wayfarer on a Sea of Fog. Hamburg, Kunsthalle. Photo Elke Walford, Hamburg.

page 13 – Albrecht Dürer (1472-1528): Large Turf. Vienna, Graphische Sammlung Albertina. Photo Scala Archives.

Mechanical toy of the 1920s in the shape of a grasshopper. Yokohama, Teruhisa Kitahara Tin Toy Museum. Drawing by Lorenzo Cecchi.

page 14 – Paul Klee (1879-1940): Landscape with Yellow Birds, 1923. Private property. Photo Hans Hinz / Artothek. © Paul Klee by SIAE, 1999.

page 15 – "The Beautiful Forest," a miniature from a manuscript of the Carmina Burana. Medieval German art of the 13th century. Munich, Staatsbibliothek. Drawing by Lorenzo Cecchi.

Central part of a shield, in gold, depicting a stag. Scythian art, 7th to 6th centuries B.C., from the kurgan (burial mound) of Kostromskaya in the region of Krasnodar (Russia). St. Petersburg, The Hermitage. Drawing by Lorenzo Cecchi.

page 16 – Carved leaf-shaped dish, in tortoiseshell, depicting a landscape with two birds sitting on a branch. Japanese art of the 19th century. Private property. Drawing Studio Stalio / Sauro Giampaia.

page 17 – Henri Rousseau (1844-1910): Jungle with Jaguar Attacking a Horse. Moscow, Pushkin Museum. Photo Scala Archives.

pages 18-19 – Katsushika Hokusai (1760-1849): Wave at Kanawaga, colored woodprint from the series "Thirty-Six Views of Mount Fuji." Photo Bridgeman / Overseas.

page 20 – Sandro Botticelli (1444-1510): Primavera, detail. Florence, Uffizi. Photo Scala Archives.

page 21 – Jacopo Ligozzi (1547-1632): Plant (Daphne laureola) and butterfly (Papilio Polychros). Florence, Uffizi, Gabinetto dei Disegni. Photo Scala Archives.

Painting of a fish in "X-ray" style. Prehistoric rock art, Obiri (Australia).

After a copy by Charles P. Mountford. Drawing Studio Stalio / Sauro Giampaia.

pages 22-23 – Justus van Utens (16th century): View of the Villa of Pratolino. Florence, Museo di Firenze com'era. Photo Scala Archives.

page 23 – Gold rose. Medieval art of the 14th century. Paris, Musée de Cluny. Drawing Studio Stalio / Sauro Giampaia.

pages 24-25 – Jean-Baptiste-Camille Corot (1796-1875): Souvenir de Mortefontaine. Paris, Louvre. Photo Scala Archives.

page 25 – Mosaic of a wolf attacking a stag. Medieval art of the 11th century. Reggio Emilia, Museo Civico. Drawing Studio Stalio / Sauro Giampaia.

pages 26-27 – Ivan Rabuzin (b. 1921): My World, 1962. Zagreb, Gallery of Modern Art. Photo Scala Archives.

INDEX

animals 4, 5, 8, 13, 14, 15, 17, 21, 25
artists 7, 8, 9, 11, 12, 13, 17, 24, 27

birds 4, 5, 8, 14, 16
Botticelli, Sandro 20

carvings 16
colors 7, 9
Corot, Jean-Baptiste-Camille 24
Cross, Henri-Edmond 7

drawings 8, 21
Dürer, Albrecht 13

fields (meadows) 9, 20
figurines 4
fish 8, 21
flowers 9, 20, 23, 27
forests (woods) 11, 14, 15
frescoes 5
Friedrich, Caspar David 12

gardens 22
grasses 13

habitats 4
Hokusai, Katsushika 19

Impressionists 11

jungles 17

Klee, Paul 8, 14
Klimt, Gustav 9

landscapes 12, 14, 16
leaves 16

miniatures 15
Monet, Claude 11
mosaics 25
mountains 7, 12

oceans (seas) 7, 15, 19
ornaments 8

paintings 5, 7, 9, 11, 12, 13, 14, 17, 20, 21, 24
photographs 17
plants 4, 5, 17, 21, 22
ponds 5, 11
prints 19

Rabuzin, Ivan 27
Rousseau, Henri 17

scrolls 5
shapes 8

tortoiseshell 16
toys 13